AF479958

Thank God for the imagination.

Thanks to my family for the support and patience.

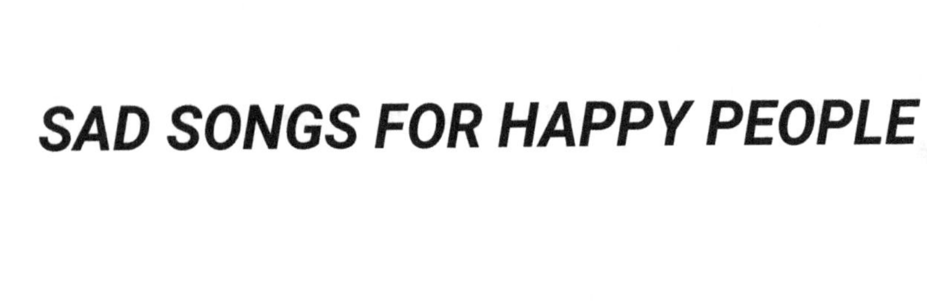

SAD SONGS FOR HAPPY PEOPLE

AN ARTIST............6

ON SET..................9

HEY THERE, GOD.....11

THINGS WE'D TELL THEM (WHILE THEY'RE STILL HERE)....15

US KIDS.................16

TOUR DE REVENGE: PART I........18

4 CHORDS & A BROKEN HEART........21

KNOWING ME.........23

WHAT DO WE TELL THE KIDS?.........25

ONE MILE FROM HOME........27

REMEMBER IT MOST DAYS.........29

WHO HAS YOU.........31

THEM PUNCHES...........33

TO THE SKY.............35

FISHING................36

WHY SING.................37

9/12............39

QUIET NIGHT.............40

DIFFERENT SUITS.............41

WHAT COMES AFTER.............42

EVER LIVED................43

THAT FAMILY ALBUM..................44

SOMEONE I LOVE IS GONE.........45

LINEAGE...........46

DEAR MOM AND DAD (LOVE YOU FOR A LIVING)....47

KING BED...........48

SEE IT TOO..........49

RIGHT THERE...........51

WHERE I AM..........52

FARTHER DOWN.........53

THERE GOES OUR 20'S............54

TEARS AFTER MIDNIGHT.............55

CLOTHESLINE......56

REWRITE......58

SECOND STRING.........60

EVERY PART OF YOU............62

TOO HEAVY..........64

UNION STATIONS............65

FAVORITE SONG.........67

THE TIME LEFT WITH THE ONES WE LOVE.............69

HE ORDERED A PALOMA.............71

RED HATS.............73

SLEEPING ON AIRPORT FLOORS............78

I CAN'T STOP.............80

I MISS..................82

THE FRONT DOOR.................83

ME AT 17...............84

AREN'T WE LUCKY ONES...........87

CHURCH GREETER............89

HOTEL ROOM.............91

YOU BUILT ME, I BUILT YOU..........93

GOD OR A GOOD TIME.............94

GOD AND I...............96

THE MAN YOU HAVEN'T MET...............97

HOLES.............99

ALL ALONG.........101

FINGERS TO THE BONE...........103

DEBRIS STILL...............105

WISHING WELL..........106

EMPTY MANSIONS............107

BRIGHT SIDE...........108

GO ON, GET THERE..........110

THE LAST ONE IN THE PICTURE............111

TOOK A BUS...........113

GOLIATH..........115

ATLAS'S DILEMMA.........117

THIS IS LIFE.........119

TRULY LIVED............122

HAUNTED HOUSE IN HOLLYWOOD........123

WHAT IT ALL MEANT........125

COMPLIMENTARY COFFEE......126

COVERING SHIFTS......127

COLD WATERS PART I.......129

NEVER TOO LATE........131

HOW MANY GOODNIGHTS......133

MAV......135

SORRY FOR YOUR LOSSES...137

HOW YOU HEAL.......140

"An Artist" (Revisited)

I'm an artist to the full extent
So if I fail there goes the apartment
There goes the ability to eat for a week
And meeting up with friends
Who can afford the parking
Keep my head down and order water
They're celebrating life and downing vodka
I guess the hardships make
The accomplishments grow fonder
Just wondering how can I go much longer
They're waiting for me to do something big
Had a few large interviews
Have been waiting for something since
Shout out to my friends just checking in
I got my bank statement
Lord, I need some saving

I'm an artist to the full extent
Pulled apart by anxiety and debt
In the business of dealing with pain and regrets
Ending our days with tears and cigarettes
Spent a paycheck on an outfit that fits me
Filled the tank to cross the whole city
Called a day off and asked the boss to take pity
Just to get to the audition and the casting acted shitty
I'm an artist to the full extent
Another gig lost, there goes the apartment
Can't eat with the stars, I'm starving
Can't look at my parents' faces
With the pain that I'm causing

Living on a couch for a month
Let's see what happens next
Humbled by her replies on Bumble
For a guy who hasn't done much yet
"Catch flights, not feelings"
But she falls in love with money and appearance
Someone in the middle of struggle
Is not so appealing

Everyone talks to me for connections
I get it
But my day just started
Let me get through my breakfast
I want us all to win, don't call it selfish
I can know everyone in Hollywood
Yet no one's investing

I'm an artist to the full extent
My stay here is extended
I'm not a roommate, just a long term guest
My friend's patience is impressive
Told him he's the first on my list
To thank when I've made it big
Rolls his eyes since it's the fifth time
I've said it since meeting him
And just when I think it'll turn around
Wake up to find myself
Six hundred dollars down
Everyone thought by now I'd run this town
Turns out I'm just running myself into the ground
And that ground sees me laying face down in mud
A mix of doubt, sweat, tears, and blood
Just when three hundred hits the account today
I lose double that on some autopay

I'm an artist to the full extent
And my arms have reached as far they can
Family has things to take care of now
But I can't help without throwing in some towels
All this time and nothing to my name
Somehow got a loan to look up some planes

Booked the flight for tomorrow, it's time to go
Flirting with my mid-30's
With a 420 credit score
Started on a high but ending on a low
Just when I get the call someone wants to buy
Something I wrote

"On Set"

Fifth month filming on set
Thinking of dad back home sick
My sister's about to give birth to twins
And I'm supposed to keep it all in
A room of creative souls need their checks
But who's checking in on me five months in?
Can't keep a straight face in the scene
He's calling "cut"
I'm thinking "God please"
How can I focus on these words
On these pages, on these verbs
When my mind's at home
As he's battling a deadly disease

Fifth month singing in the booth
I'm supposed to be spitting bars
But I'm sitting alone in one
Sipping rum sours and puffing cigars
In a crowded room of one
Tears drying like my martini
And fists of rage pounding on the counter
Knuckles bloodier than Mary
I can't keep my voice from cracking
He's calling "run it back one"
I'm screaming "God please!"
How can I focus on these verses,
On these hooks, on these bridges
When someone I love wants to jump off of one

Fifth month sitting at the corner office
Documenting profits on paychecks
With a lot more zeros than mine
They're glaring at me like,
"What's on your mind?"
Then go off to their next task right after asking
One minute it's laughter in the break room

The minute is sadness
In front of the mirror in the bathroom
What exactly am I after?

He's emailing "finish this by 1"
I'm praying "God please!"
How can I focus on these numbers,
On these spreadsheets, on these reports
When I can barely afford to get out of this corner
By the time that I'm 44?

Fifth month in
The chip on my shoulder now a chip in my wallet
Some nights I've gone through withdrawals
And some days going cold turkey is exhausting
But here I am
Able to breathe again
Five months sober after being over it
Over the losses, over the hardships
Just to rely on a bottle
To bottle it in

I spilled it into the sink
Singing "God willing!"
My mind's at peace
Now I can focus on the moments,
On my loved ones, on these wins
And my mind is clear
From a potentially deadly disease

"Hey there, God"

Hey there, God

It's me again

Do you have some time?

I tried to dial back

But it seems you had a busy line

Callers from different countries

Different needs and different why's

I don't want to come across as needy

But I'm needing someone wise

Hey there, God

I got Psalms on my arm

Tatted over bruises

Along with some scars

I'm terrified I'll never

Get to where you are

Could you meet me halfway

I'm stuck in traffic behind some fancy cars

Hey there, God

I think I dropped from your email list

And I get so much spam every day as it is

And I'm losing connection

Not just from the internet

There's anti-virus protection

And I haven't renewed it yet

Hey there, God

I can't sleep at night

Can't figure out how I'll eat tomorrow

With a business falling far behind

Going to bed but I'm away from my dreams

Been at this every day since fifteen

Got another bill due on the fifteenth

Could use help renewing this lease

On life

Hey there, friend

Don't turn on Him

Jesus turned water into wine

Even if he won't turn back time

May you be healthy in spirit, heart, and mind

Hey there, God

I just spoke to a friend

He was on his way to the ledge

But I reeled him back in

Is there perhaps a prize to bring him to the light?

I did everything to draw the darkness away from his eyes

But I guess you've got a busy line

In the middle of my prayer

Perhaps you placed me on mute

But how can I pray when I just heard the awful news?

One day I'll smile again

But how will she pull through?

I'm pulling over to the side

To get in another screaming match with you

Hi there, God

They don't believe in you

They're not sure what I see

Even though I haven't seen you too

Who am I yelling at and

Are my praises even coming through?

Hey there, God

Call you up another time

I'm in a little pain right now

Maybe you've got a busy line

Hey there, God

I know I just checked in

Looks like you gifted my neighbor

A nice check to cash in

I don't want to rush you

But I'm feeling a little frustrated

He's getting a little sicker

When should I come back around to nudge you?

Hey there, God

On my knees again

It's been a while

Since I could breathe again

Hey there, God

Hey...

Hey.

Hey there, God

I just—

Thank you, God

For making me wait

You fed me what I needed

When I had too much on my plate

So I'm checking in, God

With plenty of things to say

But nothing comes out right

So...

Hey.

"Things We'd Tell Them (While They're Still Here)"

I saw you again when I was sleeping
We sat in the kitchen
That seat is always your seat
We had this talk before, I believe
A year before you were called to leave
On a good day I keep on repeat

I miss your laugh
I miss that warmth
And on moments I miss the mark
Would've been times you'd say
"Keep going, it's not the end of it all"
I miss our walks
I miss your hand
And how much mine would fit in yours
And on moments I missed out
Saying what I needed
I'll say them next time I'm sleeping

I heard you again on my morning drive
I turned on the radio
That song is always your song
We had this time before, I feel
But it was you behind the wheel
And we sang at the top of our lungs

I miss your voice
I miss your calls
And on moments I miss the mark
Would've been times you'd say
"Keep going, it's not the end of it all"
I miss our walks
I miss your hand
And how much mine would fit in yours
And on moments I missed out
Saying what I needed
I'll say them next time I'm sleeping

"Us Kids"

It's 5 am on the east coast
Sun setting there as I'm settling down here
The west coast has so much to boast
But I lay my head stuck on yesterday's ghosts
The best sunrise the Atlantic will see
I'm in LA barely getting scene
Everyone around has so much to gloat about
And I'm stuck without a lie to toast

It's not easy being anyone free
It's not easy being anyone
It's not easy being

When you're a kid you're coming to grips
To know you don't know a thing
When you get older
The world feels smaller
Wish you didn't know so much
When you stare too long into the abyss
It stares back into us kids

It's 12am on the east coast
What do we not know about tomorrow?
Watching the world through west coast eyes
Could it feel brighter by sunrise?

It's not easy being anywhere free

It's not easy being anywhere

It's not easy being

When you're a kid you're coming to grips

To know you don't know everything

When you get older

The world is smaller

Wish you didn't know so much

When you stare too long into the abyss

It stares back into us kids

"Tour de Revenge: Part I"

She asks me about the weather
I shot back about who's been texting her
It's not my business anymore
Four days later
Then I decided to not choose torture
Took down the pictures and made some space
You're just an assistant in the art department
And I saw your true colors way too late

The boys said they'll pick me up at seven
"Bring a bat and some champagne"
I'll never run for President
But they said I've got a war to campaign

I'm trying to fight it
I'm not one for hate
But I love revenge flicks way too much
To not retaliate

Don't call it a tour de revenge
It's just a reckoning with a few car wrecks
Heartbreaks make us famous
And I'm cashing in some checks

Broken glass, painted words
What do I tell my ex's parents
It's their house and not hers
And I truly like Ruth and Clarence
Oops, they are bound to be casualties
Folks who found it in them to love me casually
They're catching stray bullets
Yes, I pulled it
But hey, they'd get in the way naturally

The boys rolled out after eleven
Popped the trunk to hide the evidence
And if ever run for President
Tell the world I wasn't present

I'm trying to fight it
I'm not one for hate
But I love revenge flicks way too much
To not retaliate

Don't call it a tour de revenge
It's just a reckoning with a few car wrecks
Heartbreaks make us famous
And I'm cashing in some checks

It's so bad for my veins

No wonder I love how it tastes

Don't tell anyone, can't have them tracing me

Tie the villains to the tracks

Trainlights piercing through the black

I'd be easier to catch but no one's replacing me

Who's gonna love you after me?

You'll get sidetracked by a new Taylor album

And the new man will love you passively

I guess that's the best revenge

When it's no longer me

This isn't a tour de revenge

It's just a reckoning with a few car wrecks

Heartbreaks make us famous

And I'm cashing in some checks

"4 Chords & A Broken Heart"

I guess you were never mine
And maybe I was on your body but not your mind
They showed me the redlights
But I didn't see the signs
Stringing me along, I took six strings
And wrote some lines

My words are my defense
Caught me in the wild armed with nothing but a pen

They found me by the weeping willow
Flowing my watered eyes
I had some time to fill up
Not knowing where I'd sleep that night
I suppose it's how it starts
4 chords and a broken heart
I can't remember the last night I slept
When that's my pillow but not my head

This week deserves vodka on ice
The boys came around to give me advice
Told me it's time to replace her
I gotta drink it straight and no chase her
I'm bending over backwards to be kept around
She's bending over forward for half the town

Her words are her offense

Caught her in the wild with nothing but a camera lens

They found me by the weeping willow

Flowing my watered eyes

I had some time to fill up

Not knowing where I'd sleep that night

I suppose it's how it starts

4 chords and a broken heart

I can't remember the last night I slept

When that's my pillow but not my head

They asked me how's my mental state

I said California

They replied, "You saw the signs

We tried to warn you"

Pursuit of happiness

I just want to be content

She's more concerned

With the followers

And uploading content

They found me by the weeping willow

Flowing my watered eyes

I had some time to fill up

Not knowing where I'd sleep that night

"Knowing Me"

Six pack, six figures, six feet tall
He's the devil
I've got the track record of an angel
He's not at my eye level
Work our way through strangers
Just trying to find our way to heaven

Thought you'd be different but hope's a novelty
Going through a phase like the rest of the scene
Your legs are as open as 9:15

I mass messaged everyone and no one texted back
Maybe it's just me or that's today's fad
In a world like this maybe loneliness ain't that bad

They say the worst and best things come in 3's
And we know the third strike hits home differently
Is she a red flag or perfectly green to me
Some days you wish we never met
Most days you wished you never left
Many nights I wish to forget
Spend your nights chasing him
You have more standards than there are straight men
He's too narrow to know your playlist
Maybe we're both music and you played us
You can find us on Pitchfork or Faded

I know you'll never be mine
In a time of abs and jawlines
Just a guy enjoying simple nights
A few drinks and poetry
He's the in to all the parties
If that's where your heart is
It was a pleasure knowing you
Maybe someday you'll get to knowing me

I can't get a reply but her stories paint a picture
The presentation's pretty like all the faces with her
Table's full, no empty seats at the dinner

I'm not entitled, just thought it'd be nice
To get the chance to charm you
Without having to pay the price
I tell others to move along but I can't
Take my own advice

I know you'll never be mine
In a time of abs and jawlines
Just a guy enjoying simple nights
A few drinks and poetry
He's the in to all the parties
If that's where your heart is
It was a pleasure knowing you
Maybe someday you'll get to knowing me

"What Do We Tell the Kids?"

What do we tell the kids
We tried the treatment but the disease won't quit
They're too young to know the half of it
Honey, what do we tell the kids?

What do we tell my dad?
To borrow bucks for breaks we cannot catch
Been at it for years but this chance may be our last
Honey, what do we tell my dad?

Life won't come easy and faith won't come cheap
Words make it all real the louder we speak
We expect our eyes to take it with ease
We break it to everyone else
But what do we tell ourselves?

What do we tell the girls?
Their brother just tried to leave this world
He isn't the only one who hurts like this
Honey, what do we tell the girls?

What do we tell our friends?
Is it our pride that won't let us get the help?
Been burning the candles at both ends
Baby, what do we tell our friends?

Life won't come easy and faith won't come cheap

Words make it all real the louder we speak

We expect our eyes to take it with ease

We break it to everyone else

But what do we tell ourselves?

Before I break it to you

What do I tell myself

"One Mile from Home"

Just a mile from home
When the tires screeched
When the glass shattered
When two lives convened
Just one mile to go
When the car karaoke
Turned into screams
Now no one speaks

They say just one mile from home
Guilty on the heart of the driver
Hangs heavy on the bartender
Hangs heavy on the bar
Hangs heavy on the friends
Who saw him before he got in the car

One mile from home
They sang to the radio
Now no one speaks...
Feels like a dream

And now she's alone to pick up the weight
Painkiller, please kill her pain
Riding solo in her lane
One baby in her arms, one more on the way

They say just one mile from home
Guilty on the heart of the survived by
Misery on their minds as they drive by
Hangs heavy on the one who found them
Hangs heavy on the one who called the kin
Replays the moments he talks to them

One mile from home
They sang to the radio
Now no one speaks…
Feels like a dream
And now they're alone to pick up the weight
Painkiller, please kill their pain
Two sides detoured in their two lanes
One mile from home
They sang to the radio
Now no one speaks…

"Remember It Most Days"

Time for the holiday dinner
Call out to the squad
Playing ball out in the front yard
As she stares out the window
With eyes just as empty
As the gift my ex sent me

We're all in on it
Play pretending
She doesn't know what the year is
Force of laughter through the seriousness

She'll look at my face
And remember it most days
She think it's hers
On all of her worst days

Say a prayer for our loved ones
All those here and gone
Blessing the food on the table
But not a minute too long
Because she'll look up from her praying hands
And not remember why we're there
Gathered around the kitchen table
With triple the servings and double the chairs

She'll smile for a moment
Because everybody made it home
And that moment comes and goes
The happiest minute she'll ever know

She'll ask where grandpa is
And she'll ask again in five minutes
No one has it in them
To tell her it's been ten years since

And she'll smile for a moment
Because everybody made it home
And that moment comes and goes
The happiest minute she'll ever know

Then she'll look at my face
Remember it most days
Blessed that tonight had its moment

"Who Has You"

Spoke to a prophet who said I'd never make a profit
But my dollars will come in the form of a girl
So I saved up my dimes in case I ever met a dime
And one day I finally came across her

A packed room, a quarter till two
Everyone parted like the Red Sea
I was seeing hues, white and light blues
The moment she laid her eyes on me

But I knew the second I had you
Was a second counting down

Late nights staring at the fire light
Thanking God it's me you warm up to
Then it hits like a chill in the dead of a night
I'm the one man in the world who has you
But I'm the one man who can lose you too

Spoke to your mother, she told me all that bothered you
Wrote a list of what to avoid
You spoke to my brother, and soon you'd discover
Everything that brought me joy

But you knew the second you had me
Was a second counting down

Late nights staring at the fire light

Thanking God it's me you warm up to

Then it hits like a chill in the dead of a night

I'm the one man in the world who has you

But I'm the one man who can lose you

"Them Punches"

They promised you sunshine
And left you with rain
Told you a longer runtime
And then the credits came

You rolled with them punches
And took those jabs
You fell in the dirt
And managed to laugh

You promised them five minutes
Right before the traffic jam
Saw fifty missed calls
Just as the plane lands
You rolled with them punches
And took those jabs
You fell in the dirt
And managed to laugh

Drowning in the deep end
Searching for a reason
To come back up
Gasping for air when
You realize that
Trying is better than luck

Days like these when

You just want to leave it

It doesn't all add up

But stick around for the aftermath

And take those jabs

You fall to the bottom

And come right back

"To The Sky"

They all see her on the screen
Fans and friends alike
She has endless potential, it seems
A list of men at her knees
From the dirt to the sky

Sex sells, that's the easy profit
Exactly what is the loss margin?
And can they stick around skin deep
To spot the beauty underneath
That stretches from the roots to the sky?

They all see her on the screen
One day this could all be behind her
But every page on the internet age has their reminders
Of the list of men fallen to their knees
Looking up at her towards the sky

The love part, is it economic?
Is there a margin of loss and profit?
A man to come along in full stride
Bury his tibia in dirt to hold her high
From the screen to the sky

"Fishing"

Early morning waking
Right before the sun breaks
He shakes me from the bedside
And we fill up all the trunk space
With coolers and fishing rods
And thank God for the day
Before we head out to the lakeside town

I'm no fan of the smell
Or the salt breeze chill
But you love it so I do it still
Hour after hour and we've got no catch
Not here for the fish but the memories attached
Find your spot and cast your line
You love it so I joined you that time

It's 5am again
And there's coffee on both our breaths
Drunk and sore from the long night before
And I'm completely spent
The winter air is too cold to bare
But I don't want you going alone
It's dark out there
The ocean has reached our hair
And I've got a series to binge at home

I'm no fan of the smell
Or the salt breeze chill
But you love it so I do it still
Hour after hour and we've got no catch
Reeled in the bait and shared a laugh
You try again and cast your line
You love it so I join you every time

"Why Sing"

Why sing of heartbreak
Where's the fun in all that?
I could use a break
And I've got a heart to match
We could fall in love
But I've better luck to fall in debt

Your favorite song plays when you enter the tunnel
Sing your heart out but bad girls
Fall in love with the drummer
Finally found "the one" but she ends up a runner
Why sing?
Well, maybe someday there's a silver lining
Hiding behind the blackest of skylines
Pain is what they all know best
When the words come rhyming
And maybe someday there'll come someone
Who'll let the sunshine in
And that's when you'll realize
Why you sing

Then you go through it again
Losing someone who knew your tone
You could use a break
From having your vocals strained
But there's a beauty in the pain
That's what you've heard them say
You're turning over that stone
Learning to be on solid rock again

Your favorite song doesn't sound like it used to
Sing your heart out but the world
Seems to turn down the volume
Finally found "the one" to build you up
Only to ruin you
So why sing?
Well, maybe someday there's a silver lining
Hiding behind the blackest of skylines
Pain is what they all know best
When the words come rhyming
And maybe someday there'll come someone
Who'll let the sunshine in
And that's when you'll realize
Why you sing

"9/12"

Nothing more American than 9/12
Turning estranged neighbors into friends
Just like how the movie begins
It takes a funeral for the boys to be boys again

Nothing more human than shared pain
Turning a stranger into a familiar face
Songs of veterans and sacrifice
Then carry on with life come 12/9

There's nothing more American than
Someone else's war mission
But there's nothing more Christian than
Handing out forgiveness
And if we can share this nation with
Those who wronged us
Even when their grandpas bombed us
Then who am I to stop us from reconciliation

Remember the day before 9/12?
We stood together and time stood still
Raised our flag firmly in hand
"This is love, and I love where I am"
Then at some point the wheels roll once more
Strangers who were friends just before
Are moving along to the beat
Of a new world

Maybe that was someone else's mission
To bring us together through division
And if there were bombers
Who kept the peace like the treaty promised
Then who am I to stop of us from reconciliation

Nothing more American than 9/12
Putting our differences on the shelf
Just like them TV friends
It takes a funeral for the girls to be girls again

"Quiet Night"

Everyone's on an evening out
We're spending the quiet time at home
You're eating chocolate kisses after dinner
And I'm kissing on your collarbone

Having fun while still dressed
I guess it really is love then
Some will label it wholesome
All I know is you make me whole

Everything's at the club dropping a thousand
To send an image to those around them
You're watching reruns on the net
As my temple rests where your arm and chest connect

Having fun while still clothed
Your body a monument no other man knows
Some will call it boredom
The longer I wait, the more I'll explore

Everyone's wondering where's after hours
Still time to take someone home
Do you miss being free as a college kid?
Or want me here kissing on your collarbone?

Having fun with no attempt
To get you out those clothes
We're in control of what comes next
On this quiet night at home

"Different Suits"

Billionaire woke up to a cancer scare
His money couldn't heal him
Poor man woke to the billionaire on TV
Wishing he could be him

They pass each other on the street
Busy on their phone lines
One running late to his meeting
The other seeing his mother one last time

Made their way to hospital rooms
The poor man there all day
The rich man not free till 2
One man's mother hanging on
The other man stuffed with tubes

His room right next to hers
Same doctor, same view
They suffer the same disease, just wear different suits
Walking the same mile in different shoes
One in Payless the other in designer boots
Two people on the tail end of this passing through

Then one day the news breaks
The son brings her a bouquet
The treatment's working
And it's time for her to go home
The rich man has just a few days
Praying for a miracle to come his way
Because the treatment isn't working
And there's no one to carry him home

They pass each other on this earth
Walking the same mile in different shoes
She learns to bury her past pains
He's buried in designer boots

"What Comes After"

The red carpet isn't everything
Looking forward to the little things
Little me's and wedding rings
Thinking of what comes after this
With a girl who believes we'll be together
Even when our bodies end
Is that too hard to get?

Who needs Hollywood
When you can have a happy ending this good
Watch stars swarm the country sky
As we lay there on your car hood
The numbers aren't everything
Eighty thousand likes from men
Who'd never offer wedding rings
Honey, what comes after this

Your twenties you put in all you had
And you lost just about everything
For a thirties that shouldn't feel this bad
Filled with empty tanks and emptiness
Go home to mom and dad every now and then
There's no shame in missing where you started
The fears, the dreams, the anxieties
A test to see where your heart is

And the red carpet isn't everything
Looking forward to the little things
Little me's and wedding rings
Thinking of what comes after this

"Ever Lived"

Fighting God for something He never did
But He gave us the greatest man who ever lived
Some of us wish to be 18 again
Others thank God 19 came
I try to be someone who joyously gives
But my art often feels derivative
How can I be a change to the world
When the nickels I earn don't make much sense?

Fighting God for something He never did
But He gave us the greatest man who ever lived
Some of us wish to be 21 again
Others thank God 22 came and went
I strive to be somebody different
But my body's started to feel much different
Haunted by scars delivered
By an other who's no longer significant

All of these factors pushing me backwards
But maybe it's me keeping me here
Everybody around me trudging through molasses
But they're moving forward
Leaving me here

Screaming at God for something He never did
Forgetting to praise Him for everything He gives
Judging my friends for not staying back here
But how can you blame them
For cruising by while I am anchored?

Fighting myself for something I never did
On the brink of becoming
Someone I can forgive
If I get older simply existing
Then did I ever truly live?

"That Family Album"

Faded Polaroids in a family album
You can count the years but never the outcome
Some born in homes, others never got one
Thank God he's outdone Himself with this one
There'd be more pages but the thing with aging
Time is something you can never outrun
We keep on going, going, going, going
Then it's all gone
Time is something you can never outrun

Another Polaroid added to the page
Some do it for the memories
Others do it for the stage
These are the nights!
Downing forty's in the parking lot
With the best people you've ever wanted
Adding another candle to the cake
Life is a short trip, doing 40 in a 35
Some of us waiting for a new arrival
Others grateful we ever came
We keep on going, going, going, going
Then it's all gone
Time is something you can never outrun
It keeps going, going, going, then we're all done

Faded Polaroids in a family album
You can count the years but never the outcome
Prom nights and funerals
Spending long nights inside the cubicle
Missing birthdays for your first million
Missing weddings to hit a billion
You turn around and something's missing
You've got business friends but no one personal
We keep on going, going, going, going
Then it's all gone
Time is something you can never outrun

"Someone I Love is Gone"

Someone I love is gone
I'm expected to wake up and throw a shirt on
Drive to work then drive on home
Driving right when my mind's all wrong
How can I choose what I want to eat
Everything tastes the same in this defeat
They say my name thirty-two times straight
And I don't hear them till it reaches thirty-three

Someone I love has gone home
I wasn't ready for them to change address
When does the evening come?
Because this mourning feels so long
And my weeping eyes wouldn't mind the rest

Someone I love
Can't pick up anymore
And I keep calling to drop a line
It rings and it rings and it stings
When a new voice comes in
The stranger knows it's me and gently lets me cry

Someone I love is gone
When is it time to crack a joke and smile
When do I hang with the boys again
Is it ever right to spend
Money on everything we did together back then

Someone I love has gone home
I wasn't ready for them to change address
But there's comfort in knowing
Where it is we go when
It's time for us to finally get that rest

"Lineage"

Your grandma was a nurse, grandpa an artist and draftsman
You can imagine which half I took after
Fill the room with tears then kill 'em with laughter
Your mama met me when the money didn't matter
Just a boy from the 'burbs who flew to LA
With nothing but a dream and few dollars to his name
I don't know her ring size, I don't know her face
But if you're reading this then it happened some day

And I'll love you like I've been loving her
Like there's no other you and there's no other her
And should the day come you have your kids
May they be proud of our lineage

Your papa was a change-maker
Your mama saw the change
Some saw me beautiful
Some saw me strange
And I didn't ask her on a first date
Until I knew her heart was in a good place
I don't wear the face of many men
And she still saw a pure soul even then
Uncles were the best men you'd ever meet
Auntie is the woman you'd want to be

And I'll love you like I've been loving her
Like there's no other you and there's no other her
And should the day come you have your kids
May you give them what I'd give

Just a boy from the 'burbs
Who sought to change the world
With nothing but a dream
And few awards to earn
I don't know her ring size, I don't know her face
But if you're reading this
Then it happened some day

"Dear Mom and Dad (Love You for a Living)"

Dear mom and dad
I'm sorry
Taking longer for me to live out this dream
Chasing an industry that isn't chasing me

Dear mom and dad
I'm sorry
Wrote a list of countries we'd see
But I'm scared this dream will outlive me

They're ten years younger than I am
Ten times richer than I am
They picked up a camera and figured it out
From the comfort of their hometown
I chose to conquer big cities
Where even the ugly ones are pretty
Picked up a pencil and hoped I figure out
How to make six figures by now

Dear Mom and Dad
Wish I could I love you for a living
Then by now we'd hit a billion
But if a book was published and no one read it
Was it ever written?

Dear mom and dad
Turning those sorries into one-way tickets
We can go wherever you want
And be happy for a living

Dear mom and dad
And to my siblings
One day these plans will pan out
And we'll know what it's like living

"King Bed"

Morning coffee doesn't feel like it used to
She pours three sugars when she knows I like two
And the sun doesn't rise the same way
With the curtain closed
And her pillow in a different place

We share a king bed
But it feels like long distance
A few good fights
Turn into long nights
And nothing feels the same
Somehow we've drifted
Treading the same water king bed
We're facing the same direction
But there's no telling where we're headed

A stranger stopped me on the street
And asked how I'm doing
I said "I'm doing fine"
I couldn't stop for conversation
But he read between the lines
There are wars and corrupt politics
And much far worse things
But I can't focus on bettering the world
With a battle on the homefront
And stepping on some mines

We share a king bed
But it feels like long distance
A few good fights
Turn into long nights
And nothing feels the same
Somehow we've drifted
Floating the same water king bed
We're facing the same direction
But there's telling where we're headed

"See It Too"

Had one hell of a day at the 9-to-6
Ready to drown my lips in liquor
At the end of my shift
Any hour is happy if I get in my sips
Whiskey and ginger thrown in the mix
Free parking after 6

I stare up and it's already midnight
Could've sworn I'm more sober than this
I'm over it
At least I said that last night
And then I saw her

Of all the dives she walked into mine
She reminds me more of steak dinner and wine
How could she possibly want
A guy drowning in Miller High
She saw me at the corner booth
Come last call approaching 2
Of all the dives she walked into mine
If she sees something in me
Then maybe I should see it too

I stare up and it's already day time
Could've sworn I'm more sober than this
I'm over it
At least I said that last night
And then I saw her

Of all the dives she walked into mine
I'm slowly shifting to the deep end
As shallow as I am five drinks in
She's the face of an angel
Inside a pub in Hell's Kitchen

Maybe she's here to save me
Bravely
Pulling me up from my beer-laden button down
But who am I to tell you of her face
I can't see it straight
She punches in her number so I can
Chase her now

Walks me outside, clutch to her arm
Tighter than her purse
I tell her about my week
With a round of thoughts
Mixed in with slurs
Driver pulls up and I can't wait
To take her home
She tosses me in
I love the aggression
I black out and wake up alone

Of all the dives she walks into mine
I fell in love with the idea
Of something divine
Thought she was there to save me
From myself
Just to save my dollars
From more bottom shelf
Of all the dives she walks into mine
Saw my next lover but she saw
A stranger in need of help
Maybe it was an angel in the dive
Who stopped me from wanting to drive

"right there"

Not everything works out how we plan
And that's the way it works
Hoping for a year from now
If we get through eleven months first
I can love Jesus and never see His face
No, not in this time and place
Not everyone works out how we want them
Started off positive and now we're unsure
Leave us bruised and banged up and haunted
By the ghost of who they once were

I can love Jesus and never see His face
No, not in this time and date
Doesn't growth spawn from pain
Doesn't loss lead to gain
Tomorrow we won't be the same
And that's no defeat
12 circles back to 12
No matter which way you read
The grass is green
Right there at your feet

Keep getting broken-hearted
Like it's an art form
I'm the artist and the buyer
Can we keep it on layover?
I can pray to God and never hear His voice
But listening is a choice
The wait is over
Doesn't growth spawn from pain
Doesn't loss lead to gain
Tomorrow we won't be the same
And that's no defeat
12 circles back to 12
No matter which way you read
The grass is green
Right there at your feet

"Where I Am"

Somewhere between sickness and shame
I suffered the losses and bottled the blame
The earth isn't stable from where I stand
You didn't meet me halfway
You met me where I am

At the corner of SE 10th & Miami Ave
It was nothing but me and two bags
With nowhere run to and nowhere to stand
I prayed you'd meet me halfway
But you met me where I am

God, as good as you are
And as bad as I became
You didn't see me for my sickness
Or appoint any blame
Wherever I go when the wheels land
You don't meet me halfway
You come to where I am

At the corner of Sunset & Western
I didn't think anything would get any better
Just when I threw up my hands
You met me right where I am

God, as good as you are
And as bad as I think
Hands clenching vanity
Spitting blood in the sink
A seat at the table
Right where I stand
You didn't meet me halfway
You met me where I am

Somewhere between sickness and shame
I suffered the losses and bottled the blame
The earth isn't stable from where I stand
You didn't meet me halfway
You met me where I am

"Farther Down"

Sitting here playing pretend
But nothing's going right
The bar back was not so tender
When I told him about my night

Went into details about the pain I've been around
He said the upside to hell is
You can't get much farther down
I can't get much farther down

Some fool pulls up next to me
Losing pool three times in a row
Orders six shots for right now
And a side of headache to go
Went into details about all his debts around town
I said the upside to hell is
You can't get much farther down
He can't get much farther down

Wasting so much on Uber money
Someone come pick me up
Or give me better hours
Something to quickly lyft me up
But I'm drowning in in the bottom half
Of this Dixie Cup
High in social status
But low in self esteem
Parking wasn't the only thing
Needing validation
Gain of clients and loss of patients
And my team has sat here waiting
Went into details about the pain that's been around
He said the upside to hell is
You can't get much farther down
I can't get much farther down

"There Goes Our 20's"

I woke up 34, but I was just 23
Selena just a hit a billion
And I can't afford my next coffee
Negative in the bank
Optimistic soul
Gotta act swiftly
Do I end up breaking bad or flat broke?
There goes our 20's, cash and age
I swore I had plenty
Years and change

I woke up in the yard
But I was just at the bar
I can't find my friends
And I can't spot my car
Back to the venue
Where I left my card
One look in my eyes and they
Said to forget the charge
There goes our 20's, cash and age
I swore I had plenty
Years and change

Woke up to my neighbor
Who just went viral
I slept on my followers
My posts went silent
Thousands of dollars
Each day from their posts
Maybe I'm wearing too many wrinkles
And way too much clothes
There goes our 20's, cash and age
I swore I had plenty
Years and change

"Tears After Midnight"

The best dinner laid out for us
All smiles at the table
The kids run off to their screens
Life as simple as it seemed

He had it all laid for us
Never thought he wasn't able
The lamp stayed lit on the nightstand
And gas always filled the family van

Somehow we had what we needed
Even if he was left defeated

The kids tucked in and mom's asleep
You try to stay in bed but you cannot dream
Sneak into the kitchen for your favorite drink
When you hear a sound around
The corner and take a peek
He's balled up on the couch with papers in a pile
Something happened to his dinnertime smile
Stare from the other room and realize
It's the first time
You see daddy cry
His tears after midnight

"Clothesline"

Started looking older but I'm not looking back
Got lost in Angeles with just my shirt and backpack
I'm not a ten, it shows on every test
Bitter pill to swallow more effective than my meds

She got used to airing her dirty laundry
Had a change of heart with
The changing of her sleeves
She saw me once and immediately
Turned to leave
Not knowing in five months she'd
Come running home to me

This year your someone else's Valentine
Chances are we'll meet in July
Months after he leaves you high and dry
Like a clothesline
You're looking at him with stars in your eyes
But then you notice even
The moon has its dark side
Then there I was standing in your eye line
This year your someone else's Valentine
While I'm sitting at home
Trying to pass the time

I can't promise forever but I can promise for now
Will you write a song about me
If we dissolved somehow
Maybe not think that far ahead
Don't gotta write down the vows yet
You're not seeing stars but
My head's in the clouds
You in the red dress
I think I'm prettier in the darkness
Pennies and nickels in my pocket but
God dropped me a dime somehow

Just know that I'm still a mess
In between work, but I'm a work in progress
At least I
Am willing to admit
I've got flaws on my face and paycheck

This year your someone else's Valentine
Chances are we'll meet in July
Months after he leaves you high and dry
Like a clothesline
You're looking at him with stars in your eyes
But then you notice even
The moon has its dark side
Then there I was standing in your eye line
This year your someone else's Valentine
While I'm sitting at home
Trying to pass the time

"Rewrite"

You've made a home here
Burn the ships
Find faith in your footing
Get a grip, would you

Strengthen your feeble hands
All it takes is a single slip
To lose everything you had
In reach of your fingertips
Could you

Tell me what is the remedy?
For a faded, short time memory?
I try, I try, I try
We cast it out to sea
Just to keep it on the line close to me
Tears dry, tears dry, tears dry
Soften your heart, start back at one
We need to walk but we try to run
Rewrite, rewrite, rewrite

We won't get this back again
Every bad time has its better end

You've felt alone here
Burn the ships
Learn to love it wherever
You get a grip, would you

Strengthen your feeble hands
All it takes is a single slip
To lose everything you had
In reach of your fingertips
Could you

Tell me what is the remedy?
For a faded, short time memory?
Retry, retry, retry
We cast it out to sea
Just to keep it on the line close to me
Tears dry, tears dry, tears dry
Soften your heart, start back at one
We need to walk but we try to run
Rewrite, rewrite, rewrite

We won't get this time again
Every bad time has its better end

"Second String"

Are these the bones you live in?
Every evening plucking at your Gibson
Singing songs, see what joy you bring them
But did you save a song for me?

Are these times we live in?
Less views than people half of my age
Half of the zeros but double the rage
But who shares the stage with me?

I want to love you but I
Won't play second string
There's a time for important things
Yeah, a time for everything
When the curtains close and
Roadies pack it down
And the fans all leave this town
You don't want to turn and see
No one left around

Look at the homes you live in
Every evening they're all just listening
Singing your songs
See what joy you bring them
But there's someone you can sing to for free

I know it's hard not to give in
Living large for a living
But even heroes lose their capes
So come on age with me

I want to love you but I
Won't play second string
There's a time for important things
Yeah, a time for everything
When the curtains close and
Roadies pack it down

And the fans all leave this town
You don't want to turn and see
No one left around

One day you'll sing out of tune
Heart sinks from the view
Of the loss of love and
An emptied room

I want to love you but I
Won't play second string
There's a time for important things
Yeah, a time for everything
When the curtains close and
Roadies pack it down
And the fans all leave this town
You don't want to turn and see
No one left around

"Every Part of You"

Here's the truth
We're not twenty anymore
We're not chasing romance
We're chasing dreams
Here's to youth
Wishing we could take back Sunday
We're going down, sugar
Maybe we'll get to love someday

But here's the truth
I'm still chasing you
Forgive me for my lack of shyness
I just wanna be a part
Of every part of you
Here's to youth

They're writing my words on their sneakers
These teens on the gym room bleachers
I should be happy but who's to say
What high is
We get paid for twenty second features
Lend us more than their small town preachers
I should be high but who's to say
Where the ceiling is

But here's the truth
I'm still chasing you
Forgive me for my lack of shyness
I just wanna be a part
Of every part of you
Here's to youth

Is this what fame is?
Even my silvers are golden plated
This is so cruel
They have me chasing dollar bills
Where's the time for chasing you

Oh, we're not twenty anymore
The music changed with the airwaves
What's romance anymore

Is this what fame is?
Even my silvers are golden plated
It seems so cruel
They have me chasing dollar bills
Where's the time for chasing you
I miss you, youth

"Too Heavy"

My dreams are too heavy for my years to hold
That's why it takes forever for them to unfold
That's what I tell myself
The more I get old
My dreams are too many for my years to unload

The adding of years and the loss of vision
It's not defeat, it's just a revision
They say to be real but I cannot listen
A difference in time, the gaining of wisdom

We try a transition to a grown up world
Where your first wishes don't always work
They were dumb anyway
That's what I tell myself
When the first year of trying turns into four

My dreams are too heavy for my years to hold
That's why it takes forever for them to unfold
That's what I tell myself
The more I get old
My dreams are too many for my years to unload

"Union Stations"

Wandered out from familiarity
Sneakers hit concrete of foreign
Emerging from depths of the Union
Into a city I've only known by name
And never by sight
These faces looks like everyone I know
Yet different
7am suits hurrying, an urgency I couldn't imagine
Off to make more money than me
A new car, a new girlfriend quarterly
Juxtaposed by a woman pushing a cart
Yet there isn't a supermarket for miles
Can't tell if the smell emanates from her cloth
Or from the holes in the sidewalk
I wish there was more room on these sidewalks
Strangers brushing against me
Different destinations, a million stories
Each with their vices and their troubles
And their worries

If only I could read their minds
To tell me of the best parts of the city
The cuisine, the views, the women
To tell of their sudden opinions about me
Of my hair, of my face
Do I look like I belong here?
Not enough room to remove myself
From this concrete square
Stare up at the skyscrapers
Who's looking down at me?
Somebody made his way up there
From this concrete square

Somewhere is where happiness lives
Searching for, yearning for
Maybe that's what I came here for
To not be home for a moment
Because home is where I stash all my baggage
But not my suitcase
Home is where we go to worry
To lay down and wonder about tomorrow
Wishing we can

Wander out of the Union Station
Pick a city, any city

"Favorite Song"

Too much on the radio
Nothing really touches me
Need something to groove to
So could you dance around with me?
Here we move in stereo
Could we waltz till about three?

There you go, red dress flows in slow motion
I'm wide awake, keeping warm
By the fireplace
We can put out the light but the fire stays

You whispered my name
It became my favorite song
All day turned into night
And somewhere the stars aligned
Pulled me close as the dance was done
Whispered my name
It became my favorite song

Too much noise on TV
Nothing really bothers me
The world cries about everything
I'm not worried about what others see
Because I'm the one who has you saved
On all of my screens

There you go, red dress flows in slow motion
I'm wide awake, keeping cool
By the window sill
Like the first time you called to me
And I froze still

You whispered my name
It became my favorite song
All day turned into night
And somewhere the stars aligned
Pulled me close as the dance was done
Whispered my name
It became my favorite song

Head on your chest
Sunrise is in our reach
I just love the way your voice
Matches the pitch of your heartbeat

You whispered my name
It became my favorite song
All day turned into night
And somewhere the stars aligned
Pulled me close as the dance was done
Whispered my name
It became my favorite song

"The Time Left with the Ones We Love"

One day when you're older
Don't forget your parents
Book them for Bali
Bring them to Paris
Build a tower of moments
And a life of memories
One day they're 35
Then one day they're 70
Holding out for another time
Thinking you have plenty

They came chasing after you
Soon as you learned to run
You walked your own way

I was two and couldn't wait to drive
But fourteen years turns mom 35 to 49
Maybe it's time to hit the stop light
Because as we get older, everyone gets older
I was young and couldn't wait to throw
My graduation cap into the unknown
Work long days at the first job you land
Then notice the pain one day in your father's hands
Get a grip on life and throw chips off shoulders
As we get older, everyone gets older

One day when you're ballin'
Don't forget your parents
Book them for Bali
Bring them to Paris
Build a tower of moments
And a life of memories
One day they're 35
Then one day they're 70
Holding out for another time
Thinking you have plenty
What are we doing
For the rest of our lives

We can choose how we spend
This not much time

They came chasing after you
Soon as you learned to run
You walked your own way
You've got a path to follow
And concrete to pave
But parents are getting older
We've got papers to sign
They were their decisions to make
And now they're mine
Prepping pills for the full week
Sunday through Saturday
First half yellow and red
Second half white and gray

What are we doing
For the rest of our lives
We can choose how we spend
This not much time

"He Ordered A Paloma"

Officer walks in with blood on his collar
And the worst look of sorrow I ever saw
Asked him what he'd like to drink
Then I stop to think
What could I possibly offer
Then he ordered a paloma
Said he'd do anything not to be sober
Says a call came in
The night came and went
And a woman died in his arms
By the time it was over

Continued to state how she looked
Like his daughter
He came for a drink but really
Needed to barter
Anything to exchange tonight's
Memory from his brain
And I was the closest man for the offer

I didn't know what to be but just be there
Sit in silence and just be there
As his salted tears flavored his rim
He holds in his screams
Wishing for the night to be over
A group of teens pass him on their exit
Glare into his soul, give him the cold shoulder
Treat him like he's one of the bad ones
Pretend to know tolerance and acceptance

I didn't know what to be but just be there
And listen as he calls his wife
He'll be coming home late tonight
Tears now streaming quicker than Netflix
Someone just died in his arms
And he has to accept it
He orders another paloma

Do I step in and cut him off
Or let him mourn in his own way
He just wants his night to be over
I didn't know what to be but just be there
Pray he finds comfort before he leaves here

Reaches the bottom of his glass
Asks for one more after that
And I
Freeze
Didn't know how to react
Throw my palms to the sky as I
Let him know I'm cutting him off
And he breaks down
He's got no partner to pick him up
Placed my hand on his shoulder
And let him weep
I didn't know what to be but just be there
The palomas are on me
He stands up from his bar stool
"The one thing I signed up for
I didn't do"
Has to face the world outside
Who already view him as cruel
And he couldn't catch the criminal
Of the woman who died in his visual
Maybe the man who saves
Needs some saving too

He passes another officer on his exit
Another night of serving, defending, protecting
His soul beat and eyes red as the neon sign
Wears a stern face but there's no pretending
Speechless as he reaches the counter
Outside he's stalked by reporters and cameras
Wishing for the evening to be over
Takes a seat and asks for a paloma

"Red Hats"

I pushed them away and for what?
Called them crazy, called them extreme
It took some time and I joined the team

They keep talking about abortion
When a million people just crossed the border
Not all of them are evil but of the portion of the people
Just committed murder
And when you can't afford anything
At the stores anymore
Voting for someone just because
She has two X chromosomes
At the expense of restoring order
Hollywood is all supportive
Of course though, they don't feel the impact
Of inflation, they can't relate to the working class
Just trying to get a paycheck
That makes sense out of their dollars
Blind when no one can cross over
Their ten foot fences
They don't know about the fathers
Who just lost their partners
Killed by someone who trekked much farther
But go ahead, you get paid for pretending
For a whole summer
A family's business is boarded up
And when it went down in flames
You applauded
Piss off, Hollywood
Bailed out the arsonists
In the middle of lockdowns
When parents couldn't feed their
Sons and their daughters
And guess which ones raised funds
To actually build them back better

Turning people into martyrs for merch
Turning a profit from faces on t-shirts
Whose families don't see a penny
That they were promised
But some people bought large mansions
No wonder the right wing expanded
Our grandfathers voted the same way
For 60 years expecting change
What's the definition of insanity
They said four letters was white supremacy
They told me conservatives were the enemy
And claimed liberals were the friends
At least they pretend to be
Wait till they see who half of us voted for
And that'll be the end of it
We'll lose "all our rights"
But there must be confusion
Because what rights are we losing?
Ever been in a relationship so abusive
When they tell you you've got
The freedom to choose
But only leave you
One option for choosing?
Want me to hate him so bad
But how can I hate someone
When I never knew him
Tell me I'm licking boots of
The enemies who keep hurting
I've got a reasonable mind
But if 99 sheep stay in line
And I'm crucified for straying
Then exactly who's doing the herding?

For four years I was running from
Another four years I saw where they're coming from
Lied to till my face turned blue
Took some time but I threw on a red hat on too

I pushed them away and for what?
Called them crazy, called them extreme
It took some time and I joined the team
Now I finally see what they've been telling me

Four years ago
I voted for her
Now my daughter's murdered because
Of an open border
I can't say a word
Because I'd be labeled a traitor
But she couldn't even me a call
To express condolences
You think I need some persuasion?
Policy over personality
Media will immediately
Paint me as a betrayer
Of my race even though race
Is no longer the first thing that matters
In these races
Calling everyone racist
Throwing every -ist at everyone
We no longer know what
The word's definition is
If something benefits America
It's good for me too
No matter how dark my face is
And the anchors ridicule a character
No matter what good he does
And they'll attack his supporters
Because of a flawed perception of him
Take a five minute clips and turn into
Five seconds without context
And it'll turn you against
Your family and friends
And you'll skip Thanksgiving
Meanwhile the presidents
Who spent their time campaigning against
The man in charge before him
Are now all meeting up for breakfast

If the leaders of two wings
Don't even think that low of each other
Why the hell did you just block
Your best friends?
You fell for it
If he's really "literally Hitler"
Then why wish him well
Instead of wishing him dead
When a bullet flew inches from his head

Why shake his hand on live TV
For the world to see
On the debate stage
If he's really as evil as you frame
Here are the keys
Take care of the House
Let's transition peacefully
Is not something you say
To someone you actually think
Is a dictator
At the inauguration
They'll give him a standing ovation
To show America healing
But that's not something you do
If you truly feel he
Is a fascist

Try to enforce us, send reinforcements
Of celebrity endorsements, we've been so poor,
They said they've been for us
Force us to put something in our bodies
Or we couldn't go
To the grocery stores
The other side said
Take it if you want
And the other side said
Take it or you wouldn't have a job
And the same corner store
Doesn't exist anymore
The same guy who stole
Seven hundred dollars in liquor
Kept coming back for more

Security couldn't stop him
According to the law
And the business couldn't survive
The state of California
Guess we couldn't see
The trees for the forest

For four years I was running from
Another four years I saw where they're coming from
Lied to till my face turned blue
Took some time but I threw on a red hat on too

They tell me this side wants me dead
Or they don't support me
But 75 million includes
My cashier, my mechanic, my doctor
My friend of ten years
People who never wanted
The worse for me
But the other side does
75 million includes
Strangers on sidewalks
Who ask me how my day went
Men, women, and children
Who care about the basics

Told you to wear a mask but
Love how French laundry smells
Told you to stay home home but
Had to fix her hair and nails
The world came to town so we
Cleaned the streets for the football game
Said it's okay to hold our breaths
With others in the picture frame
The networks forgive the hunter
But demonize the pray
Tell us we're their neighbors
And remind us we're enemies every day
Control the colleges and the knowledge
Spewed on their view
But lose it when others don't view them
They call for healing but they create
The same old divisions with a new sum

I pushed them away and for what?
Called them crazy, called them extreme
It took some time and I joined the team
Now I finally see what they've been telling me

"Sleeping on Airport Floors"

Heading into arrivals
Tired minds know the flow
Crashing at A5
Finding my sense of home
Thinking of all the times B4
Wherever it is I belong
Sleeping on airport floors
Forever yours
Is this my sense of calm?

They're asking me where I'm going
How do I respond?
I left my dream in one city
And my heart lives in another one
They ask me where I'm from
Is it the place I etch my name on stone?
They ask me where I'm going
As if I'm ever really gone

Finding a couch as the wheels touch down
Another place where artists go to roam
Broke dreamers tired but sleepless
Up against a million and one
Another morning, another coffee
Another brewing storm
Sleeping on airport floors
Forever yours
Is this my sense of calm?

I'm off to another rental
To finish what I started
In a month I'll finish writing
But I left my passion before departing
So here I am again
Another morning, another coffee
Fiddling with this pen
Pretending to finish what I started

I'm searching, I'm looking, I'm longing
For what? Who's to say
Off to another town and
Maybe this time I'll stay
Play the part of laughing with locals
Maybe they'll get my jokes
Instead of thinking I am one
And maybe I'll make this home

Instead of sleeping on airport floors
Never yours
Finding a sense of calm

"I Can't Stop"

I can't stop drinking alcohol
I could've sworn I had thick skin
Then I looked in the mirror
And caught myself wrinkling

The clock turned into something
I don't recognize
It went from midnight to sunlight
Just as I blink my eyes

I can't finish you now
Place you in the fridge
See you in another hour
Once I down all my meds
Saving you for later
But it's killing me
And I pray you keep your flavor
I was water once
So can Jesus turn me into wine
Or will I end up drinking myself?
He can give second chances
But can't turn back time

I don't need water
I'm russian over to the vodka
I'm a different person
Yelling at everyone I love most
Walking out the door
I'm not a goner but I'm a ghost

Maybe I'm sobering up
Maybe just sober enough
But maybe I'm close to the edge
Choking again
On words not spoken up
Just maybe if I ask for help
I can finally take a breath
But maybe if I'm pulled to the side
He'll smell my breath and the lies
And I'll stay in a cell for the night
I'm trying to sell happy
Can't you see my smile?

And sometimes I lie about sobriety
They ask me for a ride but
Google has more drive than me
I lay there, three hours at a time
Counting minutes to midnight and now
Somehow tomorrow has arrived

Finally go out with my friends
Just an excuse to press
My lips against henny
Anything to get my mind off everything
And I've been thinking up plenty
Where did all my comrades go
Looks like each has a family and picket fence
Well, if I'm alone on the weekends then
I'll pick up a six pack
Of my favorite friends

Maybe I'm sobering up
Maybe just sober enough
But maybe I'm close to the edge
Choking again
On words not spoken up

"I Miss"

You made it out of the small town
But it hits you in the come-back-around
You pursued the big city
But miss simplicity
Everyone's at the show under stadium lights
Wear your grandma's knitted sweater
When it's below 45
Nothing like summer and autumn nights
Around here
Thank God ma and pa found here

But I packed my life in the airplane over bin
To a city where pretty people want free things
But don't think about my overhead
I think I'm over them

I miss the autumns
Orange leaves kissing green passionately
But I'm stuck in the heat of LA
Just chasing them dreams
End of the year it calls for me
I miss the autumns
And the romance of orange falling for green
I miss the fireplace and the burning of 'mellows
I've never seen your knitting needles
Weave something so special
Keeps me warm as I
Watch the reds meet the yellows
I miss the fireplace
I miss the fire inside me

This city ain't for me forever
Maybe it's someone else's dream
Chasing numbers and chasing scenes
I wish of swinging with my niece by the oak tree
Call it a wild winter
My hands are meant to freeze
I'd rather rake all this up then to ever really leave

"The Front Door"

Sweaters in the closet bear your scent
Even though I've tried my best to bury it
Every hand I've held since you left
Don't have the same wrinkles and crevices
The longer you live the more you lose
A door with different people stumbling through
There's no way to come back to you
There's no pain like someone gone too soon

If you had to leave, then leave
But you took a piece of me
Who put the exit sign
By the front door?
And if you go, just know
It'll be a while to find
Some peace in me
I'll live good so that someday
I'll meet you at the gate
And enter through the front door

I hear the tears run beneath your breath
I haven't washed the sheets where you wept
Not a single wrinkle and neatly kept
Hoping you come back to lay your head
I can pile it with the mess
Mix it in with the rest
But I'm scared that I'll lose your scent
And remind myself you ever left

If you had to leave, then leave
But you took a piece of me
Who put the exit sign
By the front door?
And if you go, just know
It'll be a while to find
Some peace in me
I'll live good so that someday
I'll meet you at the gate
And enter through the front door

"Me at 17"

Hey you
It's me at youth
You're curious what all of this means
We were all just kids
Why's it feel like
Our breaths get replaced
By demons thumping out the chests?
Young and restless
You won't know it yet
But the world doesn't end with
A few failed math tests
And you'll notice one day that
No one's sleeping at 2 a.m.
Screaming into pillow cases
As if no one reads it on our faces

You're scared and you're reckless
You hung your halo on the hat rack
And you're hell-bent
You can care less about the lessons
Written in the textbooks
It's a time to drive
And find your drive
In between applications
And time with friends

And you'll experience your first losses
Grandparents and exes
Wishing you can have them all back
No matter how many wishes
They will cost you
Find things you're obsessed with
Looking at 18 and pretending that
You don't fear it
The world is different
Come midnight of your birthday
Blowing out the candles
Thinking about grandparents and exes

Life is more complex than
Figuring out your major
And acing those exams
21 hits you harder
Two decades in and you're thinking
You should be much further
And one day you'll be
The age your mother met your father
Will fate feel like regret
When you learn lessons from your losses

Hey you
It's me at youth
Take some advice and grow slower
You won't know everything
And you're not meant to
But stay hopeful
You can't control things
Like the weather and elections
And how every girl will feel about you
And how not everything's about you
Bitter pill to swallow
And also don't
Swallow all those pills they subscribed you
And also don't
Subscribe to everything advertised to you
And also
Advertise every feeling you have inside you

Hey you
It's me at youth
The earth stays spinning
What will you add to it?
You can be a politician
Half the world will hate you
You can be a singer
Half the world will hate you
You can an actor
Half the world will hate you
You can be a lawyer
And no one wants to you pay you

You'll defend someone you know is wrong
And villainize someone who's right
It'll be your job to
And not everyone you love
Will beat their disease
But you can choose to put their
Mind at ease
Nothing will be easy
Like it was at three

Hey you
It's me at youth
Trust me
You'll make it to where I am
A few misdirections on the map
But you'll give it all you have
Hey you
It's me looking back
And I'd give you a helping hand
But it wouldn't lead you
To where I am

Hey you
Just be…
It's the simplest advice
You'll ever need

"Aren't We Lucky Ones"

There's damage to the ceiling again
Thank God we've got structure
Add it to the bills
All the medication and its refills
We've got our problems
But we've got each other

Something came up at work
And there's something on my shoulders
And oh, does it hurt
Add it to the stress levels
All these pains went up several
We've got our tests
But we've got each other

Some don't call us lucky
But do they know about
What we have
With every punch in the gut
We've kept up
We came out with
Less air in our lungs
But we made it out
I'd say we're the lucky ones

We've managed to get to the new year again
Thank God we've got resilience
Because life is like
Having sky high dreams but
Living in low ceilings
We've got our problems
But we've got each other

Love is blind and you took my eyes
Your strength is something
I'll always recognize

Some don't call us lucky
But do they know about
What we have
With every punch in the gut
We've kept up
We came out with
Less air in our lungs
But we made it out
I'd say we're the lucky ones

Looking at you I know about
What I have
With every punch in my gut
I've kept up
I came out with
Less air in my lungs
And I couldn't have made it out
Without you
So I'm the lucky one

"Church Greeter"

He's got that red carpet glow
They say he's a man about town
Behind his smile is sadness somehow
Shakes hands at church
Makes everyone feel at home
But service ends
And he's got nowhere to go
Just came from church and
Already slurring off these shots and percs
It's a pain he's been paying
The pros to help bury
Who's going to lift off this burden
Can barely crack open the Bible
Because his hands know
Nothing but hurting

Then one Friday afternoon
He hangs his head down the avenue
Steps inside the cafe for morning brew
That's when he spots a face
Sadder than his
Felt compelled by God to step in
He's lost his road map
But he's got a Rode mic
Pulls out his camera
And asks for soundbites

"What do you think is missing in life?"
She looked around and said
"I can't count that high"
Two broken trying to figure it out
That's when he decided to reach out
She shot back to criticize
The look of equal pain in his eyes
"I don't want religion from someone
As tortured as me"
She shakes his hand and quickly leaves

Then one Saturday afternoon
On a weekly drive down the avenue
Spots the same man in the same shirt
And invites him to morning brew
That's when she asks
Why his face is sadder than hers
And still commits every Sunday to church
He lifted his chin without hesitation
"Faith is a journey, not a destination"
Every path leads to somewhere
And two weeks straight it led to her
Reached out his hand for goodbye
With something to think about on her ride
"Time on earth is borrowed
The difference between your and my sorrow
Is I'll do something about it
Tomorrow"

She meets him at church for the first time
Says she wants to be hurt for the last time
He told her that's not how this works
But see how Jesus works
The world will still desert you
Even if you put God first
Clarity and truth hurt
But see how Jesus works
Listened to every guru
To transform you into a new you
The world says to put you first
But see how Jesus works

He's got that red carpet glow
They say he's a man about town
Behind that frown is blessedness somehow
Shakes hands as they enter church
Makes everyone feel brand new
And when service ends
He has company for morning brew

"Hotel Room"

Staring down from my hotel room
The party on the rooftop
Maybe I can be like them
Swiping their cards comfortably
Without a second thought
Here I am on Saturday night
Writing my feelings onto pages
Hoping someday people will buy them
So I can join the party on the rooftop
And feel like them
Pacing the floor so hard
Those below me complain
I'm just trying to find the thrill again
Of writing my feelings onto pages
No hesitation
Free of road blocks and second guessing
So one day I can throw the party
Music blasting so loud I can't think
Between that and the ceiling fan
Rotating like the endless passing of time
That keeps on going without the world
Knowing my greatness
It's somewhere on these pages
If I can't offer anything, I can at least give you my words
For these phrases are lifelines to someone out there
Who needs to hear them, to save a life
If only they knew I existed
If only they knew I hear them
If only they knew I feel as they do
Looking down from their hotel room
Have you ever written gold on hotel paper?
Concierge not realizing who just walked through the foyer
A future legend, a hall of famer in the making

If only I could get out these pages
Sunday rolls in with no one in view
Everyone gone from the rooftop
That's when it hits me

Who am I comparing myself to?
After all it's an empty roof
Sit down to work on my masterpiece
Writing all day so somebody sees
Someone out there feels the same as they do
Not knowing who's above them in the hotel room

"You Built Me, I Built You"

You built me up
I built you furniture
And for a long time it was enough
At the end of it all I'm glad it was you

Now our book has seen its rearranging
Met by different strangers, different faces
And even today as we plant in different places
It's the roots that'll never be replaced

You got me here
Grateful it was you

I hope I can say
I didn't steal your good years
I made them great

You built me up
I built you a deck
Where we'd catch sunrises every morning
Not realizing something
Better is beyond horizons

Now our book has seen its rearranging
Met by different strangers, different faces
And even today as we plant in different places
It's the roots that'll never be replaced

You got me here
Grateful it was you
You built me up
And I built you too

"God or a Good Time"

She met me on my weakest nights
Drowned in Friday vibes and cheapest wines
Everything that feels good comes at a price

You saw the scripture on my wrist
Then grabbed my hand and covered it
Told me I could choose God or a good time

Just got back from double A
Doing my best out here to think straight
But with you all I see are blurred lines

Had to walk away five nights in a row
You'll use my body to win my soul
Too much of a high to feel this low
Another heartbreak, another hole
I could use a miracle
Because she's asking me to cross a line
Do you want God or a good time?

Where will I be this evening?
Thinking of her so I'm sleepless
The sweet sting of feeling needed

Just got back from double A
Looking rougher than I've ever been
I'm a gentleman so I'll crash on the floor

But you'll press yourself into my flesh
Just the tip and steal my breath
Push you off and I pray for forgiveness

You saw the scripture on my wrist
Then grabbed my hand and covered it
Told me I could choose God or a good time

Had to walk away five nights in a row
You'll use my body to win my soul
Too much of a high to feel this low
Another heartbreak, another hole
I could use a miracle
Because she's asking me to cross a line
Do you want God or a good time?

Just got back from double A
Looking rougher than I've ever been
I'm a junkie man so I'll crash on the floor

Where will I be this evening?
Am I dead or am I sleeping?
The sweet sting of the needle

"God and I"

He and I are a work in progress
It feels like I'm working for pennies
When I work my hardest
And only He knows where my heart is
But the closer I get, I feel the farthest
And round and round and
Round the cycle goes
I've felt so down that I don't know
Which way up goes
But I believe in someone I barely
Seen up close
Between God and I
I'm so imperfect
Between God and I
He can count my flaws
Between God and I
Is a bit of distance
Even if between God and I
He knows me and I
Don't know Him at all

Sometimes I feel like Frankenstein's monster
I'm drowning people instead
Of throwing flowers in the water
And only He knows where my mind is
If pretty won't fit me
At least I can kill them with kindness
And round and round and
Round the cycle goes
He lifts me up high when I'm
Thinking of myself so low
Between God and I
I'm so imperfect
Between God and I
He can count my flaws
Between God and I
I'm blessed to be known at all

"The Man You Haven't Met"

She's tired of one night stands
But fails to ever change her plans
He's sick of leaving empty-handed
Knowing they all misunderstand him
She says she wants a husband
And he just wants to feel handsome

One day they cross paths at
Somewhere they get the same outcomes
Maybe tonight will be different
If they view the room from
Different angles
He's caught by her smile
But she's staring at the man behind him
Who's not even looking at her
And already has three women with him

She finally sees him
And he's kind enough
She expected a cute meet
With some lead from a movie
For the first time she didn't
See through him
Something about his eyes
Authenticity in the black and white
She's ready to head home for the night
He kisses her on the cheek
Let's her know it's not happening like this
For the first time
A man doesn't want to get her
Naked & Famous after Gin & Fizz
And some white wine
Something feels different
Genuine

She's tired of one night stands
But fails to ever change her plans
Until a man came who wants romance
And they often misunderstand him

To be different from everyone
Who've met their ends
Like a man you haven't met
Your tears dried, you've made up your mind
You're not going back to them
You've known me for some time
But I can be like a man you never met

It's Sunday and we're sleeping in
Chest to chest
The beauty mark on your shoulder
The shape of a crest
The man who wins your heart
Takes longer to get here, I guess
The man who gets your body takes a
Friday night out with friends
But who are we to look at past exempts
Neither of us are who we were
In the past tense
Took me two years to get to this
Took other men a DM and a chiseled chin

You regret your past choices
But at least it's led to me
And for the first time
In a long time
It no longer gets to me
I've been here this whole time, it seems
Hidden behind the starting team

Your tears dried, you've made up your mind
You're not going back to them
You've known me for some time
But I can be like a man you never met

"Holes"

Holes in my heart match the holes in my logic
I start with deep thoughts but
End with shallow pockets
Where did all my money go
Chasing all these dreams
I'm wide awake pursuing
But they're running away from me

Soles of my shoes match the soul in my body
Beaten down and worn
Can't even tell you where my heart is
There's nothing harder than
Nobody seeing all this heartache
Mailed out all the invites
But no one knew about the party

Where did all my hustle go
Chasing all these dreams
I'm wide awake pursuing
But they're not waiting up for me

Then she came like a spark in the darkness
Her light shines through
A hole that reminds me
That sometimes it's me who
Routinely makes it harder
Who mixed this coal in a pile
Of all these diamonds
Just when I thought I lost the glow
I saw holes where she saw hope

Good news is I've sobered up
Even if I'm still growing up
She said reach out to God
I said my arms can't reach that far
I asked her "what's your endgame?"
She said "just worry about your pen game"

How can you dream at night
If you're stuck on the price of your bed frame?

Where did all the funny go crying about routines?
She reminded me to laugh
Even when the joke is all on me

Then she came like a
Spark in the darkness
Her light shines through
A hole that reminds me
That sometimes it's me who
Routinely makes it harder
Who mixed this coal in a pile
Of all these diamonds
Just when I thought I lost the glow
I saw holes where she saw hope

Doctor gave me facelift
But this is the body that God graced me
I can only control my character and behavior
I wasn't made to save her
I don't bare enough scars to be a Savior
I can pray for a blank slate
As easily torn as this paper

But she came like
A spark in the darkness
Her light shines through
A hole that reminds me
That sometimes it's me who
Routinely makes it harder
Who mixed this coal in a pile
Of all these diamonds
Just when I thought I lost the glow
I saw holes where she saw hope

"All Along"

I prayed to God and he showed up in five minutes
Spoke to the devil and he came in five seconds flat
Broke down to them it's getting harder to stay living
One came wearing nothing
One wore a suit and a top hat
Asked them questions to see who knew me better
One of them answered honestly
The other answered clever
After an hour of pressing them
Everything got settled
I asked God to stay and sent away the devil

Told him everything on my mind and when I finished
He stuck around and I played him a song
I asked God what took him five minutes
He looked me in the eyes and replied
"I stood behind you all along"
All along
All along
He looked me in the eyes and replied
"I stood behind you all along"
All along
All along

Next day came and I asked God to come back
It felt better than speaking to
The man in the suit and top hat
Had a million more questions on top of that
But when the moment came
I stood silent and fell flat

Then screamed at Him in agony
I lost my job and all my friends are gone
He looked me in the eyes and replied
"I stood beside you all along"
All along
All along

He looked me in the eyes and replied
"I stood beside you all along"
All along
All along

The devil got lonely and looked for company
Found me grieving by a weeping willow tree
Tried to make me believe and
Told me I was too blind to see
That's when God came around
To send devil right back down
I had to rub my eyes and
God cured me of my blindness

Cried out to Him in confusion
Where were you to right these wrongs?
He looked me in the eyes and replied
"I've stood before you all along"
All along
All along
He looked me in the eyes and replied
"I've stood before you all along"
All along
All along

"Fingers to the Bone"

Works his fingers to the bone
Four hours left till home
Smells of oil, sweat, and dirt
And the bills won't stop piling up
Pulls up to his drive
Can't look his wife in the eye
Sits alone for hours
All he wants is a cold one
He can't say who he'll vote for
In this city he's a loner
He wants who'll make things better
But they want someone who's nicer
Dad could use some medicine
And his mama's days are limited
He stares up at the setting sun
Wondering which side is brighter

Works his fingers to the bone
Looking for the hope to hang onto
But the skin on his fingertips grow callous
A tint of blue on his collar
Grown men aren't allowed to cry
But also get criticized
But for not showing enough emotion
In or outside his home

Works his spirit to the end
Everyone around him starts to whine
His daily earnings covers gas and it
Breaks his soul working overtime
How did the people around him
Figure out how to break out
No more shackles, no more chains
On their bodies or their brains

So he decided to save his bones
Quit the job and spend more time at home
Vacation with the family for weeks at a time
And finally work on that dream he's had
His whole life

He worked his fingers to the bone
Broke doesn't have to mean broken
Becomes the hope he's been fighting for
He stares up at the rising sun
And figures which side is brighter

"Debris Still"

I know I'm not your type
Because your type breaks you into parts
He's going, going, going, going, gone
You're left not knowing just
What the hell went wrong

They left you in pieces, debris still
Falling from the lies you
Thought were home
The thing is between us, you're still
Falling for the ones who leave you cold
A chain of regrets, you can't help but
Choose what you already know

We put you on a pedestal
Now you look down on us
Maybe we play our parts right
Timing was never my strong suit
If it was that'd be my cologne on you
Instead you smell like the best you can do
On a lonely night

They call me a good guy
But what good does it do
If I just stood by, let you fall to make believe
Before I get going, going, going, going, going
Gone
You're left not knowing

They left you in pieces, debris still
Falling from the lies you
Thought were home
The thing is between us, you're still
Falling for the ones who leave you cold
A chain of regrets, you can't help but
Choose what you already know

"Wishing Well"

Your first name and my last name have a ring to it
Even got your parents' blessing that Friday night
Counting up the years and we've been through it
And then it all changed last Friday night
A penny for your thoughts, you look lost
Care to share what's on your mind
Walked me to the well out in the yard
With a handful of pennies hoping for a dime

We threw pennies down the same wishing well
You wished to go, I wish you'd stay
I guess your coin hit the bottom first
But it feels like I'm the ones who's paying
And now that it's time to list the sale
You need to grow, I'm stuck in place
Maybe it's me to hit the bottom first
Drown in a different kind of pain

We threw pennies down the same wishing well
Held a wish the other couldn't tell
Gathering all your change for someplace else
All I can do is wish you well

Your first and last name removed from the statements
Even your parents' have me changed in their phones
Counting up the times I thought we'd be better
Now the address on the letters
Reads a different "Sent From"

We threw pennies down the same wishing well
You wished to go, I wish you'd stay
I guess your coin hit the bottom first
But it feels like I'm the ones who's paying
And now that it's time to list the sale
You need to grow, I'm stuck in place
Maybe it's me to hit the bottom first
Drown in a different kind of pain

"Empty Mansions"

She wants men with mansions
But what's the point in twenty rooms
If they're empty anyway?
And my empire's expanded
What's the point in twenty thousand friends
If they only know my name?
I've only got two eyes but too much vision
And she's got her ears but won't listen
To her gut when it tells her
What is lust, what is love, what is left
If good men are gone, what's your right decision?

A heart with rooms the size of mansions
But no one's moving in
They're looking at homes across the city
With no vacancy signs but the yard is pretty
And she can't see the worth when she's with me
And the market's used to it
The vault's secured and the roof's protected
The outside's changed with much investment
The priest came and done his blessings
All it wants is acceptance
The vault's secured and the roof's protected
The outside's changed with much investment
There's a signal without connection

A heart with rooms the size of mansions
But no one's moving in
They're looking at homes across the city
With no vacancy signs but the yard is pretty
And she can't see the worth when she's with me
And the market's used to them
A celebrity's across the street
We throw rocks at glass homes so
We can see them
Can we just spend our night staring at stars
Instead of wanting to be them?

"bright side"

You love country like me
Salty when you need to be
but still sweet
You've made realities out of dreams
Oh, the possibilities
And maybe I feel too safe when
You're used to dangerous type of men
You see me and see nothing like them
Oh, the possibilities

You've stayed with the hurt
Unsure what is courteous
They played you like a sport
But you wore the jersey

Good guys
Putting up a good fight
And it's been one hell of a night
But I'm not changing myself
To be someone else's
Good time
Just to be tossed to the side
If you just want another lifeline
Then I'm good with being someone else's
But if you want a change tonight
I can show you the bright side

Spending your nights with frogs
You won't know what a prince is
Nature is devious
You want what you don't need
Oh, the irony
Spending your nights in beds
You barely know the owner of the bedsheets
Nature of the beast
Lying with them, wrinkles in their stories
Oh, the irony

Good guys
Putting up a good fight
And it's been one hell of a night
But I'm not changing myself
To be someone else's
Good time
Just to be tossed to the side
If you just want another lifeline
Then I'm good with being someone else's
But if you want a change tonight
I can show you the bright side

"Go On, Get There"

It's the end movie scene
Ride off into horizons
Take a breath, take a beat
You did so well
And you weren't defeated
Go on, get some sleep
We sing your praises
And, boy, it's worth repeating
You did more than good
And it's sad to see you leaving

Break out
Go on, get there
No one else owes it to you
Like you do
Find your Hallelujah
Then find your way back here

Did you pack somethings nice
The road gets a little lonely
Take a step, take a leap
You hide so well
Scars underneath your sleeves
Go on, get some miles
Ride out in style
You were it clean
We were born to watch
You were born to leave

Break out
Go on, get there
No one else owes it to you
Like you do
Find your Hallelujah
Then find your way back here

"The Last One in the Picture"

There's a frame of us that hangs by the bed
First thing I see in the morning
It's faded over time without warning
But I can still picture everyone
By the memories in my head

To be the last in the picture
I wish it was fiction
But each holiday has less of us
I pray if God was one of us
He'd ride the same bus as them
But take me home first
I don't wish to bear the losses
I spent years making wishes
And I think I've exhausted them

Thanksgiving's coming up
And I'm forever thankful
But it's getting harder to carve
And harder to pick up the babies
And my hands can't grip these knives
Like they used to
Like back in my 20's
Back when we'd go for holiday walks
To see lights around the neighborhood
Those night were good
Seeing breaths in the air
Instead of running out of them
Back when we'd plan future holidays
Because we thought we had many left

Took another picture of us
To hang above the nightstand
To glance at on night when I'm alone
When everyone's busy living
And all we get is the busy tone
There are new players in the game
With every new picture frame
To add to the legacy
Not take away from it

"Took a Bus"

I'm just a commoner
Armed with a few hundred bucks
And some street smarts
Took a bus to Fremont
Without the vaguest idea of what I'm doing
Or with anybody to leech on
Where everybody stays moving
With slots to play or a corner to preach on
I've got a few bad habits
One of them is being stuck below average
The other is hopping onto buses
Without any stops to leave on

Maybe I should've taken the Pacific Surfliner
Seattle to San D
Find a few beaches to sleep on
Pass by a few reminders
There is peace in these skies
Flying as free as the seahawks

I'm just a drifter
Taking a bit more years to get a grip
On the realities of staying in place
Finding my footing when we're intended to slip
It's always sunny in one city
Then the wind and rain sweep me in the next
She's made her mind up
So why am I still texting
I've got a heart to protect

Chasing something or running from?
What am I to expect?
I took a bus out of town
Just to avoid a major wreck

Who's down to swim in the nearest beach town
I hear the water's pristine
We can keep on drifting till sun down
But I think I have a little more life in me
Pool together change and
Buy from street vendors
Begin with churros and bottles of pop to end with
Sit back by the ocean and think of life bitterly
Or come to remember I've got more fight in me

So I book the train back to my hometown
Hitting the cafes and selling everything
The internet will allow
We can keep on drifting till sun down
But I know I've got some fight in me

I'm just a commoner
With a few bucks and some street smarts
RIght now, it's the best road I can be on

"Goliath"

This is my story
Doctor told my parents
The mission should've been aborted
Thank God for them
They didn't listen
Now my brother and I can add on to
Other people stories

Years later, grateful to report in
But the journey's hard, feels like
A resort built inside a fortress
I'm still living but it's a vision
I sense is slightly shorted
I stay breathing but my life
Could use support
They ask me for my credits but
I've got no credit to report
I'm paying the price when
I can't even afford it
What's the floor plan
For a home without a roof or a porch
Extra square footage
Just to have an empty storage

I'm supposed to be an artist
Feeling farthest from accomplished
I'm posing as a pro
But have the knowledge of a novice
Do pure hearts get you further
Or do they want someone who's polished
I've got to pimp my soul
While still searching for my solace

Ask me to be quiet
While they're preaching to their choir
They've got high hopes
I take the high road
But I'm popping all my tires
Who's responsible for the signage?
There shouldn't be a stop here
Of all these plotlines and these potholes
I can pay the fines
If I made millions from words rhyming

Crashed inside the cul-de-sac
I need a medic
But this xan is the only med I see
The shakes and anxiety
Have me fighting to say things harder
Than benzodiazepines

To think I've been on a roll
Just to not get the part
That's the biggest bitch of them all
Everyone looks at me like I'm the giant
So why does it feel like I'm facing Goliath
My pain is the biggest gift to them all
Maybe I'm a monster and human hybrid
A Philistine challenging me to fight him
But I'm slinging rocks at a mirror after all
To bare the conscience of Pontius Pilate
You can hear my answer in
The presence of silence
Pleasing everyone is my downfall

Years later, grateful to report in
But the journey's hard, feels like
A resort built inside a fortress
Mind of 25 pushing my 40's
Writing sad songs for happy people
They're mine and others' stories

"Atlas's Dilemma"

We rekindled flames just to stay warm
Wearing my suit and tie tethered and worn
The one I danced in
When we first met
Somewhere in Manhattan
Drinking Long Island's all night
Through tears and laughter
But I can tell something's on your mind
The world on my shoulders
Chin up and hopeful
But I can still tell
Something's on your mind

A second try at trying
Who says persistence has to expire
You were always about TikToks and timing
The world could see what it is I admire
You were never great at lying
I can tell something's on your mind

Here it goes again
The universe has thrown its wrench
Things align, that's what we hypothesize
Only for the momentum
To decrescendo to an end

A career takeoff like we'd expect
It takes so much of your life
If you don't take it serious
We'll both regret it
And your plate's as full as mine
Money moves has me moving soon
It's not like I can't fly
I can send us to the moon
But if I give you all my nights
Mornings and afternoons
Who's going to hold up the rest of the sky?

And who will rescue us from ourselves
Graveyard of past loves
Gave her so much spirit I lost my soul
Now she's haunted by
The father, son, and Holy Ghost
Right words, wrong tempo
She isn't ready for life changes
And I end always end dancing slow

Here it goes again
The universe has thrown its wrench
Things align, that's what we hypothesize
Only for the momentum
To decrescendo to an end

Dear Child
I can't remember lyrics
But I can remember feeling
You're like a night time drive
Safe and sound and free of lights
We all wish we were younger
But knowing what we know now
Landing softly on better goodbyes
You'll remember more than me of the good nights
Even if I don't recall all the time
You sit just fine on the swing sets
In due time the horror of time will hit
And someday I'll forget
Even the name I go by

Dear Child
This is life
We hold onto what we hold onto
That's what makes memories
All the more special
The energy flowing through us
In between the breaths
The simplicity is the effectiveness
It'll come dawning on us
That the dawn is on me
And my recollection
Of the periphery and rearview
For now I get a clear view of you
And there's beauty in that

Dear Child
I have much more to articulate
But for now we'll save them
Because there's power
In not counting down the hours and
Being in the present

The time will come when
The time comes
But I banked more years
For spending

Dear Child
Dry those waterfall eyes
It's all part of the cycle
Rinse. Wash. Repeat.
Our bodies dissipate but our
Names are infinite
And your children
And their children
And their children
Will leave an imprint
The world will speak of them
Infinitely
When you don't have the answer
Be the answer
Stop asking the same question
A million times, and just live

Dear Child
This is life
Additions, subtractions, divisions
Multiplied
This is life
Everything scares you
Nothing's fair
Pair that with the unknowing
Of when we go
The ticking of a clock
In the middle of your masterpiece
When it's time to head home

Dear Child
Think of me
But don't let me drag you down
I'm here to push you
Not keep you still
You've got dreams to fulfill
As big as the city you'll choose
To pursue once suburbia starts to bore
But don't worry, you'll miss it someday soon

Dear Child
It's never about me
It's always been about you
That's the point

Dear Child
This is life
Live it well
May you remember every step
And learn from them
Even as the albums of my mind
Open up to blank pages
Even with the scribbled faces
Fill that album up
And may you pass it on
To your Child

"Truly Lived" (Revisited)

He lost their son in a plane crash
Then lost his wife in a car crash
Couldn't deal with the aftermath
So he lost his faith right after that
It's a wonder he stood still
Instead of rolling down the hill
It's a pain you can't just pill
What comes after that?

He spent his life away from water
Too afraid to swim and get swallowed
Up by the sharks swarming
So he locked himself up in a tiny room
Nothing but a small window for a view
For many decades he existed
But he never truly lived
He spent his life away from flights
Too afraid to course through skies
Up where lighting and thunder form
So locked himself up in a tiny room
Nothing but a small window for a view
For so long he existed, But did he ever truly live?
He spent his life away from romance novels
Because maybe one day he want a story
Only to have his heart get stomped on
So locked himself up in a tiny room
Nothing but a small window for a view
For so long he existed, but did he ever truly live?
Caught his reflection, gray hair and wrinkled cheeks
Maybe now's the time to take a peak
Cracked the door open to glance outside
More beauty than his window could provide
Others swam the oceans and soared the skies
And maybe endured heartbreak sometimes
Only to end up fine, and truly lived

"Haunted House in Hollywood"

At the same premiere but you
Looked right through me
You must only like guys who actually make a dime
From making movies
And that's the funny part about the city we reside in
Getting tired from full time jobs
And getting paid like part timers

I'm on the market
But I'm labeled as haunted
Who has time to clean out
Heartbreak and cobwebs?
I came here with a thought
That girls who believe in ghosts
Would love local haunts
Maybe someday I'll be someone
Who somebody wants

Writing poems about romances I never lived
Taking chances on boxes I've never ticked
But I don't know how you're
Missing all of the fuss
I look in the mirror and I get starstruck
Yet there's a sign on the yard
That reads "hurry up please"
Every other person won't the sign the lease
Why should I pay for date night
When another man is eating out for free
It takes two to tango
And I'm far removed from the dance scene

I've been told I got a face for voiceover acting
Imagine that movie scene
Who's gonna kiss all these scars?
Who said love is squeaky clean?

I'm on the market
But I'm labeled as spotless
Who has time to teach
Love to a novice?

I came here with a thought
That girls who believe in ghosts
Would love new haunts
I want to be somebody
Who somebody wants

At the same red carpet but you
Looked right through me
You must only like guys who actually make a dime
From making movies

"What It All Meant"

She doesn't know what she's doing
All she knows is she's doing it for free
She placed first in small town pageantries
But moved to LA and is barely a three
She doesn't know what she wants now
But she knows it's the first of the month
Trying to get on yachts where
The pretty girls are
The captain takes one look
And says "we've boarded enough"

What do I get here that I don't get from home?
Anyone can take a picture and upload
What they are selling isn't good for my wellness
But they're all cheering me on back home

Her little studio is haunted by ghosts
Of actresses and writers who had much hope
There's a spot in the corner
Where the wallpaper's torn
And an old carpet a bit blood soaked
Outside the window is another premiere
A block away from a town of tents
She's just trying to get by
With her heart on the line
Wondering what this all meant

What do I get here that I don't get from home?
Anyone can take a picture and upload
What they are selling isn't good for my wellness
But they're all cheering me on back home

She sticks through a couple more years
A number of breakups and plenty of beer
But she finally finds out what it all meant
When that's her on the poster of the premiere

"Complimentary Coffee"

Plants and neon signs brighten this cafe
Everyone's laughing and I'm just hiding from the rain
Cashier glowing asking how my day went
Noticing I'm not as happy as the other tables

Then she offered complimentary coffee
Not knowing it won't lift me up
Because I just lost my best friend
Mind is blacker than the contents of this coffee mug
She tosses in a free cookie and muffin
Just to see a customer smile
But I'm living in a state of agony
And I'll reside here for awhile

How is everyone smiling
Does no one else feel the same
Maybe they're all going through it
But just at a different level of pain
Cashier asking if I'd like my coffee chilled
I'm just realizing I can't even pay the bill

Then she offered complimentary dinner
Not knowing it won't fill me up
Because I just lost my home last night
Mind is darker than the coffee that I can't buy
She tosses in a conversation
She's in need of a lifeline
Told me about how bad her day went
And we sit and talk for some time by the neon signs

"Covering Shifts"

Gotta stay up more
Working a double
Co-worker asked me to cover
His mother's in the hospital
Hasn't completely recovered
I'm yelling at him through the phone
Not knowing his struggle
Depression's got him under
Insurance has fumbled
We settled on him owing me
And I couldn't be more subtle
I want an arm and a leg
For covering his shifts
And asking an arm from his mom
When she's about to lose it

The damage has spread
How does he manage?
To keep his cool in public
And suppress all his anguish
They have to cut it off
The best case prognosis
I'm chewing him out
For asking me to close up
He's about to spend all
His money on her surgery
And about to go homeless
It's taking all the pride inside him
For me to not know this

That's when he opens up
Back against the corner
Hand against his heart
His head on my shoulder
No one to confide in before he explodes
Takes a breath for a second then he unloads
Down to the last hundred in his deposit

Can I offer some more?
He's been clean from drugs for four years
And is about to go through withdrawal
Lift his head and look him square in the pupils
"I can't speak of fortune but
don't give up on your future,
I know you're heartbroken
but keep your composure"
He soldiers on and gets through another week
I'm there for him whenever he needs to speak

Asks me to cover some nights
I'm happy to take them
His mom's gotten better
And she never gave up
A miracle for his family
Keep the money and save up
Creating more core memories
You could never replace them
He comes back to work
Forgives me for my anger and
We share a laugh in it
Glad to see a shift in his happiness

"Cold Waters Part 1"

A long day at work
He has nothing left to give
Can barely keep his eyes open
On the ride back home
When he spots a woman
About to jump off the bridge
Can barely keep her eyes open
Four hundred feet from the water below

Approaches her slowly
"There's a lot of life to live"
Walks up with arms open
To talk her off the edge
They both stand there in silence
Eyes swelling with tears
They couldn't hide them
Got up on the ledge and sat beside her
"If you jump you're not jumping alone"
She couldn't fathom a stranger
Falling into cold ocean
Knowing it was all to stop her from deciding
To jump when there's a lot of life to live

Maybe there's a reason for these two to collide
He guides her back to the sidewalk
They sit against the wall
For a few minutes to talk
He swears he's seen her before somewhere
They begin to chat about how they've both
Swum colder waters
Skeletons in their closets, a bit too honest
She just got out of prison
Fifteen years for a car wreck
Then it finally hits him

She's hopeless and homeless
Could use a place to lay her head
Her parents and siblings are gone
Everybody left her the night she went in
He thinks for a minute
His world begins to spin
The cross on his necklace
Dances between his fingers
It's almost dinner
It's time to make a decision
His road to healing detours through
Forgiveness
They hop in his car
Then it sinks in
What would his wife think?

"Never Too Late" (Revisited)

She believed all her life
Just couldn't get her husband to follow suit
Years of trying to get him to church
Were years of him not following through
How could he live in a world like this
And think miracles exist
Then came the news
His heart won't last another attack
Best to keep him comfortable

He stared his wife in the face and asked aloud
"Who is this Savior you speak of?
I could use him right now."

After 85 years he gave his life to Jesus
One month later he would leave us
It's never too late to find freedom
Never too late to find freedom

She lived her entire youth
Staring straight into the mirror
No matter the diets she put herself through
The model on TV could never be her
How could she live in a world like this
And think everyone gets happiness
Then came the day
Left a note behind for her roommate to find
Then went on her way

She stared at her doctor who pumped out the pills
"Is there someone I can listen to?
This time I will."

After three attempts she gave her life to Jesus
Just another minute she wouldn't be here
It's never too late to reach them
Never too late to reach them

He lived half his life
Sitting on 25-to-life
The things he's seen on the inside
Enough to make a preacher cry
How could he live in a world like this
And think we get second chances
Then came the news
He's getting off sooner than he thought
A second chance he better use

He stared his cellmate in the eye and said
"The book you've been reading,
I think I need it."

After prison he gave his life to Jesus
It took this long to see it
It's never too late to redeem them
Never too late to redeem them

"How Many Goodnights"

There's beauty all around us
Most of us see it only in faces
Others in how much his pockets weigh
Yet some of us in the quieter spaces
We only think of now, but ten years down
Will you be in a happier place
If you only think of now and not ten years down
When most of the beauty fades

But even if there's losing of the mind
The heart doesn't have to change

How many goodnights
Do you have till they're gone?
How many love you's
Did you have in you all along?
You meant to say it and you didn't
If things could be different, you think
But there's no gift like the present
How many sunsets do you
Have till it dawns?
What you have inside, you've had
In you all along
You meant to pray it but you
Didn't stop to think
There's no gift like the present
And there's nothing better than to exist

So much mystery around us
But I can only see in front of my space
Someone in the background
Who's been keeping me calm
I push away for a prettier face
We only think of now, but ten years down
Will you be in a happier place
If you only think of now
And not ten years down
When most of the beauty fades

But even if there's losing of the mind
The heart doesn't have to change

How many goodnights
Do you have till they're gone?
How many love you's
Did you have in you all along?
You meant to say it and you didn't
If things could be different, you think

But there's no gift like the present
How many sunsets do you
Have till it dawns on you?
You find something in him
But he's had it all along too
You meant to pray it but you
Didn't stop to think
There's no gift like the present
And life is better that he exists

"Mav"

I wonder what's on her mind
What country song slips off her tongue tonight
Studies life insurance to ensure better lives
Her smile spreads as cancerous
As her birthday sign
Born four days later she'd be a lion
She's like a spark that lights up July
Freckles line up under her eyes
She's a wonder that's on my mind

She loves her peace
She loves her thrills
I'd died a thousand times
If looks could kill
As pretty as your heart
And the words you think
I could know everything
And she'd be a wonder still

She's more than a boring nine-to-five
On most days catch her at eleven
She has more drive than I-95
Even if it's not her behind the wheel
Worked her way up to a room in the sky
She loves her Space on 11th
I could know everything about her life
And she'd be a wonder still

They meet her on vacation
And they slip in her DM's
Sometimes we wonder what's it like
If we could be them
But maybe it's better not to
Be her past men
You'd rather be her husband than a has been

Maybe she's searching for angels
But she doesn't do church like that
Maybe she finds beauty in the
Faces of strangers
But the evil inside them to drags her back
She's independent-minded
She's a mav
We all wish we could have
Someone like that

I wonder what's on her mind
What witty little quip slips off her tongue tonight
Has lived more life than others over 25
Her smile spreads as cancerous
As her birthday sign
Born four days later she'd be a lion
She's like a spark that lights up July
And even if I'm not on hers
She's a wonder that's on my mind

"Sorry For Your Losses"

Sorry for your losses
She still wakes up to the spots of blood
On her carpet
Work says take your time
School says your time
Friends say take your time
And anxiety wants to take up all her time
Months go by and she acts clean and spotless
But deep inside
She's unsure where her next thought is
Staring at the same sign at the grocery store
For the last ten minutes
Then spends her last ten dollars on two packs of cigarettes
They treat her out for coffee
Maybe a pour over could take her mind off things
She stands in line and the man she's behind
Has a sweater that says, "You belong here"
Wishes her sister could have thought this
Sorry for the losses
She still wakes up to the spots of blood
On her carpet

Sorry for the missed calls
Thank you all
But it's been one hell of a year
Mama's gone silent, papa's barely home
Things have gone sideways here
No one's talking but everyone's screaming
Trying to point the finger
And finding the reasons
Not realizing it's been four seasons
And nothing's ever going to bring her back here
But I'm fine
Keep asking me, I'm fine
Ask me again, I'm fine

The doctor prescribed something
My mind still wanders
But it's better than nothing

Sorry for your losses
I'm just checking in
I saw you smiling the other day
But something seemed a little different
Eyes were a little glossy
Maybe from the medicine?
But you stared at the same sign
A little longer than ten minutes
Could we speak in private?
You can tell me anything
Or we can sit in silence
I'm here if you need anything
Or maybe you can use the quiet
Because everyone's asking everything
Don't mean to pry but
Some things got me questioning
It's the middle of summer
And you won't roll up your sleeves
Anytime we bring it up
You get up and ask to leave
So we change the subject
I get it
We've got a body to look after
And you've got a peace to protect

Sorry for your losses
It's been a year and some change
But your heart hasn't
May I ask if everyday
There is sadness
Our bodies can leave us but
Memories outlast them

Hey, have you seen her?
It's been year two and I think
There's a breakthrough
She's smiling again but it seems different
Like she means it
I took a look at her carpet
And she finally cleaned it

She's going to her classes
And her parents are back too
She told me,
"You can let it drive you mad
Or you can let it drive you"

Sorry that I lost it
It's been a hell of two years
And we looked at our options
Nothing can replace her
But we found a few causes
To keep her memory alive
And to keep us looking onward
Hey, I'm sorry for your losses
I've been there before
Do you need someone to talk to?
I know what it's like to get stronger
It's going to feel like
The world is so wrong now
But when you a hold on much longer
You'll see it's better than being gone

"How You Heal"

Did it pierce your skin?
Has it found its way in?
Flesh and bones, heart and soul
How deep did it get?
Are you busy living
Or are you busy digging your own grave
Either way you're staying busy
Even when it doesn't seem that way
It'll hurt you then heal you
Then make you feel again
The world views a brand new you
A cup of life filled to the brim
Take a sip, every day's different
Every train returns to its station
I hope you hurt so that you learn
How you heal

You just got over it
But there's graffiti on the overpass
To remind you every bridge through
Is still dirtied from its sordid past
Are you busy living
Or are you busy being over that
Power and pain start the same
Beginning and ending has its overlaps
It'll hurt you then heal you
Then make you feel again
The world views a brand new you
A cup of life filled to the brim
Take a sip, every day's different
Every train returns to its station
I hope you hurt so that you learn
How you heal

ABOUT THE AUTHOR

Erman M. Baradi is a Los Angeles-based writer originally from Virginia Beach, Virginia. Often referred to as "Top Networker in Hollywood," Erman refers to his loyal fanbase as the "Ermantourage." He loves writing about life, hope, dreams, and the universal themes of the human experience.

"Don't spend your life thinking about how to spend your life. Just live it."